To Elin K.G.

Oi Evan! Oi Olivia! My biggest *Oi Frog!* fans J.F

HODDER CHILDREN'S BOOKS
First published in Great Britain in 2016 by Hodder and Stoughton

Text copyright © Kes Gray and Claire Gray, 2016
Illustrations copyright © Jim Field, 2016

A CIP catalogue record for this book is available from the British Library.

HB ISBN: 9781 444 91958 5
PB ISBN: 9781 444 91959 2

10 9 8 7 6 5 4 3

Printed and bound in China

FSC
www.fsc.org

MIX
Paper from
responsible sources
FSC® C104740

Hodder Children's Books
An imprint of Hachette Children's Group
Part of Hodder and Stoughton
Carmelite House
50 Victoria Embankment
London EC4Y 0DZ

An Hachette UK Company
www.hachette.co.uk
www.hachettechildrens.co.uk

www.kesgray.com   www.jimfield.co.uk

Oi DOG!

Hodder
Children's
Books

Written by
Kes & Claire Gray

Illustrated by
Jim Field

Oi DOG! GET OFF THE FROG

said the frog.

"But I like sitting on frogs," said the dog.

"Frogs are all **squishy** and **squashy** and when you sit on them they go PLURPPPPPPPPPPP!"

"You know the rules," said the cat.

"Cats sit on **mats, frogs** sit on **logs,** and **dogs** sit on **FROGS!"**

"Well, I'm **changing** the rules," said the frog.

"From now on, **dogs** sit on **logs** not **frogs!**"

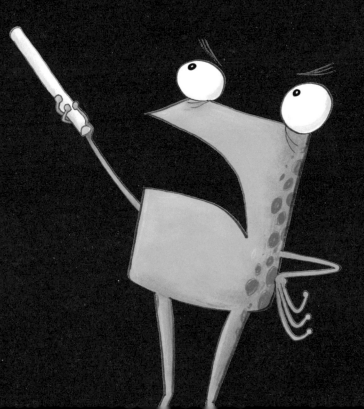

"REALLY?"
said the dog.

"REALLY,"
said the frog.

"What will **bears** sit on?"
asked the dog.

"**Bears** will sit on **stairs**," said the frog.

"What will **slugs** sit on?"
asked the dog.

"**Slugs** will sit on **plugs**,"
said the frog.

"**Slugs** will sit on **plugs**,
flies will sit on **pies**,

crickets will sit on **tickets**,

and **moths** will sit on **cloths.**"

"What will **leopards** sit on?" asked the dog.

"**Leopards**
will sit on
shepherds,"
said the frog.

"**Leopards** will sit on **shepherds,** and **cheetahs** will sit on **fajitas.**"

"You're really getting the hang of this," said the dog.

"I know," said the frog. "And that's not all...

pigs will sit on **wigs,**

Gnus will sit on **canoes,**

and **boars** will sit on **oars."**

"What will **whales** sit on?" asked the dog.

"Whales will sit on **nails,"** said the frog.

"I'm not sure the whales will like that," said the dog.

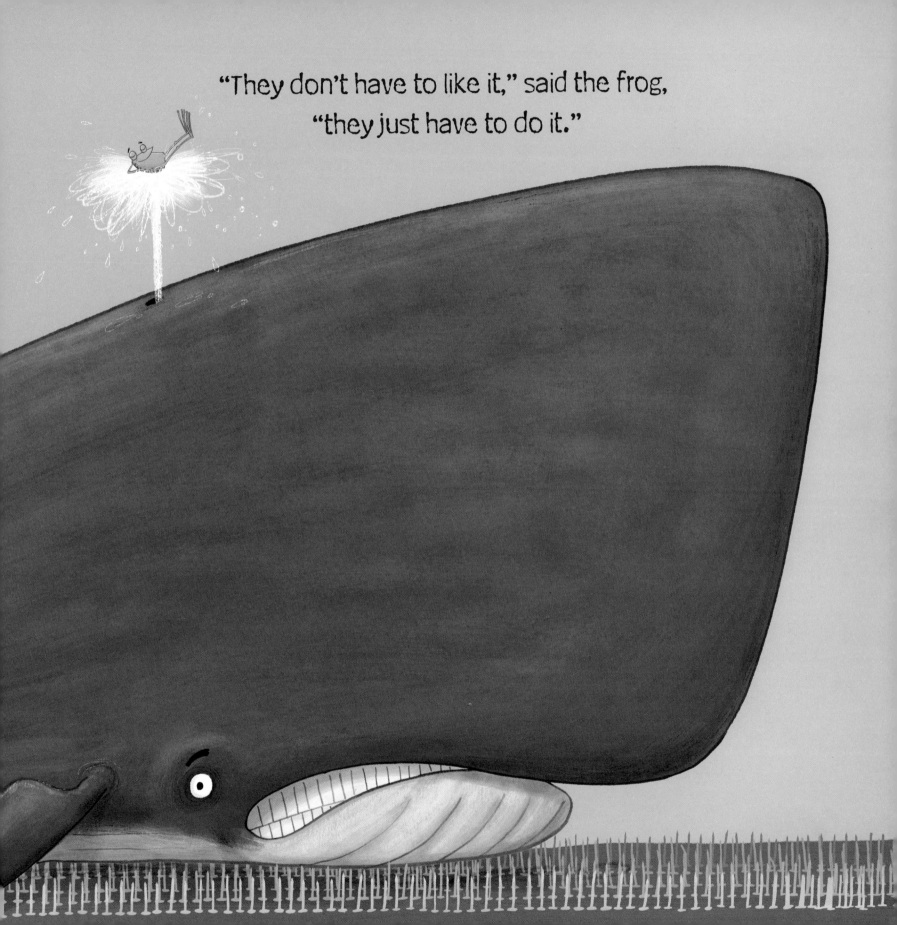

"They don't have to like it," said the frog,
"they just have to do it."

"What will **dragons** sit on?" said the dog.

ADAM'S APPLES

"Dragons will sit on **wagons,"** said the frog.

"**Dragons** will sit on **wagons**,

kittens will sit on **mittens**,

and **puppies** will sit on **guppies.**"

mice will sit on **ice,**

"What will **crabs** sit on?" asked the dog.

"**Crabs** will sit on **kebabs**," said the frog.

"**Crabs** will sit on **kebabs**,

poodles will sit on **noodles**,

hornets will sit on **cornets**,

skunks will sit on **trunks,**

and **elephants** will sit on **smelly pants!"**

"Elephants aren't going to sit on **smelly pants!"** gasped the dog.

"They are now," smiled the frog.

"Hold on," said the cat. "If **dogs** sit on **logs**, **cats** sit on **gnats**, **bears** sit on **stairs**, **slugs** sit on **plugs**, **flies** sit on **pies**, **crickets** sit on **tickets**, **moths** sit on **cloths**, **leopards** sit on **shepherds**, **cheetahs** sit on **fajitas**, **gnus** sit on **canoes**, **pigs** sit on **wigs**, **boars** sit on **oars**, **whales** sit on **nails**, **dragons** sit on **wagons**, **mice** sit on **ice**, **kittens** sit on **mittens**,

puppies sit on guppies,
crabs sit on kebabs,
poodles sit on noodles,
hornets sit on cornets,
skunks sit on trunks,
and elephants sit on
smelly pants..."

WHAT ARE
FROGS
GOING TO
SIT ON?

asked the dog.

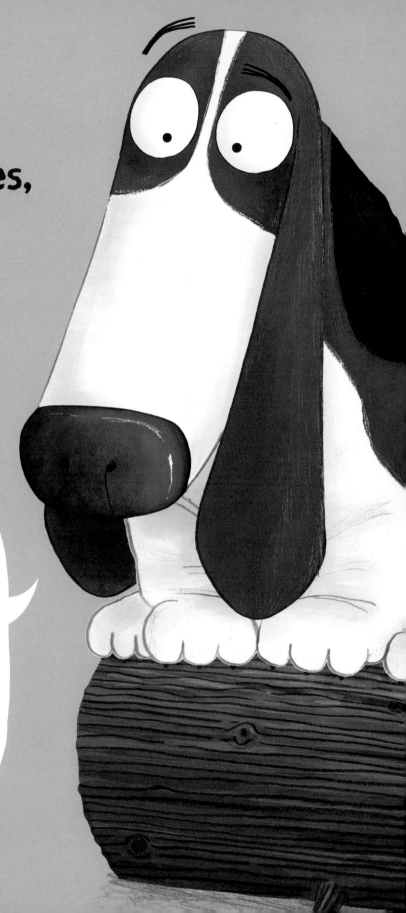